Huck Runs Amuck!

story by
SEAN TAYLOR

Art by
PETER H. REYNOLDS

DIAL BOOKS for Young Readers

an imprint of Penguin Group (USA) Inc.

For Joeyman.
–S.T.

To my goat farmer friends,
Greg Agnew Sr. & Greg Agnew Jr.
–P.H.R.

DIAL BOOKS FOR YOUNG READERS
A division of Penguin Young Readers Group
Published by The Penguin Group • Penguin Group (USA) Inc., 375 Hudson Street, New York, NY 10014, U.S.A. •
Penguin Group (Canada), 90 Eglinton Avenue East, Suite 700, Toronto, Ontario, Canada M4P 2Y3 (a division of Pearson Penguin
Canada Inc.) • Penguin Books Ltd, 80 Strand, London WC2R 0RL, England • Penguin Ireland, 25 St. Stephen's Green, Dublin
2, Ireland (a division of Penguin Books Ltd) • Penguin Group (Australia), 250 Camberwell Road, Camberwell, Victoria 3124,
Australia (a division of Pearson Australia Group Pty Ltd) • Penguin Books India Pvt Ltd, 11 Community Centre, Panchsheel
Park, New Delhi - 110 017, India • Penguin Group (NZ), 67 Apollo Drive, Rosedale, North Shore 0632, New Zealand (a division
of Pearson New Zealand Ltd) • Penguin Books (South Africa) (Pty) Ltd, 24 Sturdee Avenue, Rosebank, Johannesburg 2196, South
Africa • Penguin Books Ltd, Registered Offices: 80 Strand, London WC2R 0RL, England
Manufactured in China on acid-free paper
10 9 8 7 6 5 4 3 2 1

Library of Congress Cataloging-in-Publication Data is available upon request.

Portions of the text was hand lettered by Peter H. Reynolds. The illustrations were done in watercolor, ink and tea.

Here's a mountain goat by
the name of
HUCK.

Do you like his trendy beard?

Like most goats,
Huck will eat most things.

Cardboard boxes.

Woolly gloves.

Birds' nests.

But cardboard boxes taste like boring afternoons.
Woolly gloves get stuck between your teeth.
And birds' nests make Huck sneeze.

What he really loves to eat are . . .

FLOWERS. FLOWERS. FLOWERS.

Huck dreams of
mountain meadows full of flowers,
and mouthfuls of petals
melting on his tongue.

The problem is . . .

. . . other goats like eating
flowers too.

And there aren't any left.

Except for over there.

Look at those flowers.
Huck's looking at them.

And—

UH-OH...

he's not going to try
that impossible climb,

is he?

He is!
He can't resist!

He scrambles on the tips
of his super-grip toes.
He clambers with his knees,
his tail, and his nose.
He's up on the rock
without hesitation.
He's a clip-clopping,
cliff-hopping,
climbing sensation!

He's nearly there!
He's got one hoof on top!
His teeth are a whisker away—

But—OH NO… we've lost him!
Where's Huck?

He's tumbling...

bouncing...

sliding...

rolling...

all the way to the village
of North Polkadot.

Across the main street he comes and . . .

OH NO!

He's going to land in Mrs. Tuppleton's pond
and sink without a trace!

SPLASH DOWN!

But then he realizes the
water is only knee-deep.

And—

UH-OH... he's not going to eat
Mrs. Tuppleton's flowery underpants,

is he?

He is!
He can't resist!

He scrambles
on the tips
of his super-grip toes.
He clambers with his knees,
his tail, and his nose.
He's up on the clothesline
without hesitation.
He's a high-kicking,
back-flipping,
climbing sensation!

He's nearly there!
He wiggle-waggles his tail!
His teeth are a whisker away—

But– OH NO!
It's Mrs. Tuppleton's
German shepherd dog!

The clothesline gets
in a spin.
Huck jumps.
He hopes
for the
best . . .

VOOF VOOF
VOOF
VOOF VOOF

and lands
in a pile of
boxes outside
Mr. Hartwig's
General Store.

Huck takes a big bite of a box.
It tastes like boring afternoons.

But look! What's that?

UH-OH... Mr. Watson has bought
some flowers for his wife.
Huck's not going to try to snatch them,

is he?

He is!
He can't resist!

He scrambles on the tips
of his super-grip toes.
He clambers with his knees,
his tail, and his nose.
He's up on the bridge
without hesitation.
He's a clickety-clackety,
climbing sensation!

He super-grips his toes!
He reaches down!
His teeth are
a whisker away—

But— OH NO ... a train!

It gives Huck such a shock
that he tumbles onto
a boy on a bicycle.

He hopes he's got the flowers
between his teeth . . .

. . . but Huck's disappointed.
He's got something else.

Now what's this? It's Melissa Spooner's wedding!
Everyone is ready for the family photograph.
But what does Huck spot?

The flowers on
Mrs. Spooner's best hat!

UH-OH... he's not going to climb
that hedge and eat them,

is he?

He is!
He can't resist!

He scrambles on the tips
of his super-grip toes.
He clambers with his knees,
his tail, and his nose.
He's up on the hedge
without hesitation.
He's a sneezing, wheezing,
climbing sensation!

The photographer's ready!
Everyone's smiling!
Huck's teeth are
a whisker away—

But—OH NO!

A gust of wind
has lifted Mrs. Spooner's hat
high into the air.

"My best hat!" she cries
as it lands atop the church spire.
"If only somebody were
brave enough to fetch it!"

But Huck isn't listening.
Those flowers look tasty—

and he can't resist!

He scrambles on the tips
of his super-grip toes.
He clambers with his knees,
his tail, and his nose.
He's up on the church spire
without hesitation.
He's a lurching, perching,
climbing sensation!

Will he make it all the way?
It's harder than he thought—
The spire has slippery sides!

Huck glances down.
All around, people are peering up at him.
There's Mrs. Tuppleton.
There's Mr. Hartwig.
There's the Watson family and the Spooners!
Everyone is urging Huck on—
even the German shepherd dog.

"He's going to rescue the hat!"

"That's one big heart in one little goat!"

"VOOF! VOOF! VOOF!"

The people seem so proud of him!
Mrs. Spooner looks so pleased!
Huck's teeth are a whisker away—

And—OH NO...

What are they going
to think if he *eats that hat?*

BUT HE DOESN'T!

A cheer goes up!
Huck turns around.

The hat is in his mouth!

Huck gives the hat back to Mrs. Spooner—
without even a nibble at the flowers!

She is so delighted, she invites Huck
to the wedding party on
the village green.

It's a perfect occasion.
Birds are singing. Butterflies are fluttering.
A five-tier wedding cake sits on
a flowery tablecloth.

And Mrs. Spooner says to Huck,
"You can eat just whatever you like."

So he does.